Mama Said Keep Your Dress Tail Down

Olivia M. Dutton

This book is a work of fiction and does not depict any person living or deceased. The characters and events were created from the imagination of the author.

Mama Said, Keep Your Dress Tail Down

Is the first published work

Of

Olivia M. Dutton

Copyright © January 2014

Book 1

Mama Lou ~

**Mama used to tell me, "Girl, just you keep livin';
you don't know nothin' about life. Just mind your P's
and Q's, and don't be no fast tail girl."**

I didn't much understand exactly what a fast tail
girl was when I was growing up. She used to tell me all the
time if I didn't listen to her, I would become one. I loved
my mama, but I thought she was a little soft in the head.
She always had all these sayings; sayings that made no
sense to me, seeing as I was a child. But when I became a
full-grown woman, I began to understand—the hard way.

I'm Mama Lou; that's what everyone calls me and
have been, since after I had my second child. I don't rightly
remember who gave me the title or how or why it stuck, it
just did. I think it might have been my Aunt Johnnie Mae.
She said I'd become an old soul in a young body after all
that had happened to me.

I'm lying here on my deathbed, after nearly sixty-
four years of wading through the troubles of this world. I
didn't think I would leave this earth so soon, but what can
you do? Cancer came calling and decided to stay. I should
have known though. It took Mama out much earlier than

me. So I guess you can say I was blessed to have a few more years.

My children keep peeping in here at me like they expect me to get up and fly away. You know, like that old hymn we used to sing in the church. I may be feeling poorly, but I ain't right ready to leave this plane of existence just yet. I have a few things that I want to say, to leave behind, in hopes it might help my granddaughters. Lord knows I tried to give my daughters this wisdom, but they didn't take to it. Those girls always thought I was trying to rule their lives or something. But that wasn't the case. I just wanted them to avoid the pitfalls I found myself in during my life; especially when it came to men. My mama may have been a little touched in the head, but she sure was right. I just wished she would have been better at teaching me these things, instead of speaking in parables like Jesus did in the Bible.

The Early Years ~

Growing up in rural Mississippi, there wasn't much for us to do, but work the fields and play around in those same fields, when we weren't working them, which wasn't often.

I was ten when my mama insisted that I wear dresses all the time, even when we were gathering crops. She said young ladies should always look like ladies. No man wanted a woman who dressed like him. I often wondered about that. How would mama know what a man wanted? Hers, my daddy, ran off before I turned two and she never had another one since—well, not one to keep anyway.

Before I turned ten, I was allowed to wear pants like the boys. I liked the pants, because I could run and jump in them, and never have to worry if my dress got caught on twigs in the woods. But Mama put a stop to all of that on my tenth birthday. She had one of the neighbor women to make me three dresses, which I wore until they couldn't be patched no more. I wore those dresses even when I began to grow out of them. Mama would just let them out and add more material to the bottom of them. Sometimes when we were in the fields, I would purposely tear the added-on part off, hoping Mama would let me have my pants back. It never worked though. She would just add it right back on.

When the work was done, I would run from the fields to play. I preferred playing; running through the woods or the corn stalks, hiding from the boys. Mama never liked me playing with the boys and always tried to discourage it. I didn't understand why. All we were doing was playing, and mostly hiding and seeking. Whenever she caught me running through those fields, being chased by those boys, she would holler for me to come in the house. And when I got there, she would pull me aside by an arm and say, "Girl, always keep your dress tail down. Don't let those boys get the better of you."

Mama never explained what she meant by that, never did. As far as I was concerned, she didn't have to worry about me keeping my dress down. I would look real silly walking around holding it up. We were poor and most of the underwear I wore was patched, because they had been washed so many times they had become holey. So there was no way on God's green earth I would want anyone to see those patched-up holes. That's why I thought Mama was a little touched. Her sayings just didn't make no sense.

When I got my period, mama had a new rule for me. I was never to be alone with any of the boys I used to play in the cornfield with. I asked Mama about this, and she just said she didn't want to have to rock no babies that weren't hers. I didn't understand what my period and playing had to do with babies.

I asked her how do you get babies and Mama got all nervous, mumbling about how I would find out when I got older. Well, I got older, but she never really told me. I used to talk to my best friend Eva about things my mama wouldn't tell me; like where babies came from, and she would shake her head and say, "Girl yo' mama ain't taught you nothin."

One night, I was sleeping over at Eva's house, when we heard noises coming from her folk's room. Eva got up and beckoned for me to follow her. We snuck outside and ran around to a window that looked into her folk's bedroom. There was Eva's daddy, Mr. Albert, naked and on his knees. He was hovering over an equally naked Miss Sue, Eva's mama.

Miss Sue's titties were uncovered and jiggling when she moved about. Miss Sue's titties were big. My mama always said it was a sin and a shame that Miss Sue had such big titties. Well, from where I was standing, Miss Sue had those titties, especially for Mr. Albert. He liked them, he liked them a lot. I watched him take them in his hands and lick all over them. This seemed to make Miss Sue very happy because she tried to push more of those big things into his mouth.

After a while, Miss Sue started moaning and wiggling around, when Mr. Albert got tired of the titties, he produced something long and black from between his massive thighs. I had never seen anything like that before. Eva whispered she had seen that thing lots of times when she would sneak out to watch her daddy and Miss Sue. She had even seen it when she caught Mr. Albert on top of Miss Lucy, who lived down the road. Miss Lucy's titties weren't nearly as big as Miss Sues though.

That black thing that was attached to Mr. Albert, attached between his legs, was huge. It looked like a big strong stick. I wondered what he was going to do with it. Was he going to hit Miss Sue with it? He didn't seem to be mad at her or her at him. When it started to quiver some, move on its own, he grasped it in his hand and stroked it a bit, maybe to calm it? This seemed to make Miss Sue real glad because she smiled and opened her legs wide. When she did this, Mr. Albert took that thing and stuck it between her thighs, inside of Miss Sue.

Whatever that big thing was, it was making them both moan and wiggle around. Mr. Albert was a big broad man and to watch him rut around on top of Miss Sue was mesmerizing. He was pushing and pulling, making grunting sounds. Whatever Mr. Albert was doing, he started slow at first, and then he got faster. His big body moved like I had never seen a man's body move before. And Miss Sue? Well, she started moaning louder, wiggling more, as he poked and pulled that thing in and out of her. Then Mr. Albert asked Miss Sue did she like his big dick.

So that was what that thing was called. Miss Sue answered, saying his dick made her pussy feel good. I didn't understand what Mr. Albert's dick had to do with Miss Sue's one-eyed cat, Mabry. That cat always tried to scratch me when I played with it.

Later, when Eva and I got back to her room, I asked her what was that her folks were doing. She said they were trying to make a baby. I didn't understand; and I didn't understand why watching Eva's folks made me feel all funny inside, mostly between my legs. I had to fight the urge to put my hands down there and press. After that first time I witnessed Eva's folks rooting around, I began to spend more nights with her. I wanted to have that feeling again.

Older Now ~

I got older, but Mama still didn't tell me nothing. I felt like I was left out of the loop on everything important and getting dumber.

As I got older, mama made me stop playing with the boys altogether. It didn't matter if I was alone with them or not; I just couldn't. Mama also made me stop spending so much time with Eva. She said that girl knew too much, and no good would come to it. I couldn't hang around Eva and I couldn't play with the boys, what was I supposed to do?

Mama also made it plain that I was to stay away from Eddie Joe Collins. He was one of the older boys that lived in our town. She saw how I was grinning at him one day when we were in town shopping for food, and had a hissy fit. All I did was giggle at something he said, but it was enough to push Mama over the edge. She grabbed me by my arm and hauled me out of that store. She didn't say anything, but I could tell she was mad because her lips were all pursed up. Mama never hit me before that day, but as soon as we got home and got inside the house, she slapped me hard across the face. She apologized later but told me not to ever forget it though. She never explained why she hit me. It was like always, when it came to important stuff, I was left out of the loop.

Later that day, mama had to go back to the store, because she was in such a hurry to get me home to slap me, she forgot the flour she needed to make the pies for the church picnic. Still smarting from the slap she gave me, I feigned sick to keep from going back to the store with her. While she was gone, I wanted to study on why she hit me awhile. I didn't figure it out until much later.

Mama hadn't been gone five minutes when Eddie Joe came knocking at our door. He had come to deliver the apples Mama had paid him to pick from his family's apple orchard. Eddie Joe was older than me; a couple of months from being twenty years old. Mama said he was a man, and no young girl should be dealing with a grown man. I was fifteen but didn't see much difference between us, other than he was a boy and I was a girl.

Eddie Joe was what the older women, (mama's age), called a fine young buck. All the girls in the area vied for his attention and some of the older women did too. He was tall and muscular with skin the color of smooth chocolate; the kind mama let me eat sometimes. I say sometimes because she said chocolate would make my face break out if I ate it all the time. I think I only ate it sometimes because Mama really couldn't afford it.

Anyway, getting back to Eddie Joe. He knocked on our door and asked if Miss Taffy was home. (Miss Taffy was mama). He was holding a big bushel of apples she had paid for. I told him Mama wasn't home. Mama always told me to never let anybody in the house when she was gone, but seeing as she had already paid for them apples, I didn't see any good reason for Eddie Joe to have to come back a second time, so I let him inside.

Eddie Joe followed me into the kitchen where he placed the apples on the table. I was sort of grinning. I couldn't believe it. Eddie Joe Collins was standing in my kitchen looking just as fine as ever. Then I remembered the last time I grinned at him and stopped.

After he placed the apples in the kitchen, he followed me back into the sitting room. I was heading back to the front door when he grabbed me by my hand and pulled me to our shabby, but clean couch. He wanted to sit for a while and talk. I wanted that very much. But what I didn't want was Mama coming home and catching Eddie Joe in our house. I was sure she would hit me again. I guess that was a chance I would have to take.

At first, we did talk. Wasn't much; just about things that happened around town. Then we started playing, with Eddie Joe tickling me and me laughing. Before I knew it, my back was on the couch, with Eddie Joe stretched out on top of me. He started rubbing his lower body against mine. While he was doing this, I could feel something hard pressing into my "special place", as mama called it; that place right between my thighs. Then he sat up, and with me watching, he unzipped his pants and pulled out what looked like a brown stick. I recognized what it was immediately. It was a dick like Mr. Albert had. Eddie Joe's just wasn't black like Mr. Albert's, but it looked just as big.

He asked me if I had ever touched one before. Eyes wide, I shook my head no. Eddie Joe took my hand and wrapped my palm around it tight like. It felt hard and slippery. He used my hand to work that thing up and down. While we were doing that, Eddie Joe's eyes rolled back and he started making those sounds I heard Mr. Albert make. The more he moaned the faster we worked it. After a while, we stopped and something came squirting out of it. All of a sudden it wasn't big and hard anymore, but small and soft. I snatched my hand back. I didn't know what to make of the change.

I watched while he stood up, took a rag out of his back pocket, and wiped up the stuff that came squirting out. After he was satisfied that he was clean, he tucked himself back into his pants and zipped up; putting the rag back in his pocket. "You ain't ready for the real thing yet," he told me. He leaned over; he kissed me on the mouth and left.

I sat there stunned at what just happened. I was still sitting there when Mama came back. I thought she would get mad when she walked into the kitchen and saw those apples sitting on the table. She asked me about them, and I told her Eddie Joe left them on the porch, and I brought them in. To my relief, mama seemed satisfied with this and started moving around the kitchen, making her pies. Eddie Joe never came back to our house after that, at least not when I was there. He never got a chance to show me the real thing.

#

A few months later, mama came home throwing up her hands and shaking her head; talking about how she knew no good was going to come to that girl knowing so much. She had just found out Eva had a baby growing inside her, and Eddie Joe Collins had put it there. She told me to stay away from that girl because she was fast and a bad influence.

I thought about this a bit. Eva had been sneaking out of the house during the night, but not to watch Mr. Albert and Miss Sue. She never told me where she was going, during those times. I guess she was going to meet up with Eddie Joe Collins. After all those times watching her folks, I guess Eva had the practice down pat and wanted to see if she and Eddie Joe could make a baby. She had to be better at it than her folks too, because they never came up with one.

That Sunday, mama took me to church to pray for Eva. Mama sat in that pew, bawling and moaning like Eva was her daughter. She asked God to help the poor child because life was going to get hard. I wanted to know if Eva's life was going to get as hard as Eddie Joe's dick was that day. After making me say a prayer for Eva's hardship, mama fell on her knees to say a prayer for me. Saying, "Lawd Jesus, help my child keep her knees together and her dress tail down." This was new. She hadn't ever mentioned my knees before.

Oh, and I found out later the real reason Mama was moaning and crying so, and why she wanted me to stay away from Eddie Joe. Shortly after her performance at church, I had to come home early one day from school, because of the cramps. As soon as I stepped on the porch, I heard noises coming from inside our house. It sounded like somebody was moving heavy furniture and grunting doing it. Instead of going inside, I ran around to each window, until I came to Mama's bedroom. There was Mama and Eddie Joe, rooting around on Mama's bed, naked. Eddie Joe had his dick in Mama. That same dick he had me squeeze and rub, while we sat on our couch that day. I just shook my head and went into the cornfield to wait for Eddie Joe to leave.

#

Not long after everybody found out Eva was pregnant, Mr. Albert made Eddie Joe marry Eva. Mama said it was a shotgun wedding, but I didn't see no shotgun present that day, only an angry Mr. Albert and a crying Miss Sue. Me and Mama attended Eva's wedding, along with Eddie Joe's parents, in Eva's folk's sitting room. I asked Mama, why didn't they get married in a church? Mama said what they did was a sin, and God didn't want them there.

With all the sad and mad faces, Eva's was the only one looking happy. She held onto Eddie Joe's arm tight, while the preacher said words over them and joined them as man and wife. Eddie Joe didn't look too happy about that, and neither did Mama.

Eva and Eddie Joe were only married a few weeks when Eddie Joe left going to the store and never came back. At first, everyone thought something bad had happened to him. This was Mississippi. Later we found out Eddie Joe had just run off because he didn't want to be married or be a daddy to Eva's baby. We never saw Eddie Joe again. I think Mama was more torn up about it than Eva; seeing as she was still rolling around naked with him, right up to the day he left.

You're Grown, You're a Woman ~

When I turned eighteen, Mama told me I was grown, a real woman. She said it was time that I went out into the world and find out what it was all about.

I had been working at Mr. Sims', where we traded since I was fifteen, and had saved every penny for this day. Mama had arranged for me to go up North to live with her sister, Johnnie Mae. Johnnie Mae lived in New York City and had been there ever since she ran away from home when she was sixteen. Johnnie didn't like the hard work of the South and left as soon as she could.

That day Mama put me on the train, I cried. Not so much because I was leaving Mama, but because I didn't know what to expect. She still hadn't told me much about life and even less about men. If I knew nothing living in rural Mississippi, how was I going to fare in a big city like New York?

Aunt Johnnie met me at the train station. I had only seen her a handful of times when I was younger, but I recognized her right off. She was just as pretty as I remembered. She looked like Mama, but somehow younger, even though she was older and only by a year at that. I guess the country life had made Mama look hard.

Aunt Johnnie was a slim woman, but hippy, as Mama would say. She was dressed in a color bright dress that came nowhere near her knees. She called it a mini dress. I had never seen a dress like it before. All me and Mama's dresses hung down past our knees because Mama said that's how proper women wore them. Mama would have had a fit, if she saw Aunt Johnnie dressed this way. She would have said she was half-naked.

Although I liked Aunt Johnnie's dress, I liked her hair more. It was pressed straight and hung to her shoulders. Then it turned up at the ends. She called it a flip. She wore a multicolored headband tied around it, to give it style. In her ears, she wore these big hoops that could have been worn as bracelets. Aunt Johnnie looked good; she looked rich. Those times she visited us, she looked rich then too, and I vowed I would look that way someday.

Whenever she visited, Aunt Johnnie always brought me and mama expensive gifts; sometimes clothes, sometimes jewelry. We never wore the things Aunt Johnnie brought us. Mama always stuck them in what she called her hope chest. She said those types of things didn't fit into our world and would only make people mad at us. I think she sold those things, because the day I left, she gave me extra money I didn't know she had.

As soon as Aunt Johnnie saw me, she ran to me and hugged me. She always called me her favorite being of all the people she knew, even mama. She didn't have any children of her own and was happy to have me there for company.

After gathering the only piece of luggage I had, she hailed a cab to her brownstone. I had never seen anything so grand, so beautiful. It looked like a mansion to me. It was what she called three stories in height. I was surprised to learn that nobody lived there but her. That big place was all hers.

When we got inside, my mouth fell open at the luxury that surrounded me. There wasn't a shabby couch or scarred piece of furniture in Aunt Johnnie's place, no ma'am. Everything was new and looked expensive. The windows were covered with curtains that were handmade and fancy, not homemade like Mama's curtains had been. Her table tops, in the sitting room, looked like marble. Everything was all shiny and bright, even the walls had their own color.

Since I had never been outside of Mississippi, this was all new to me. I just stood there with my mouth hung open. I had just closed it from the cab ride over, from looking at all the tall buildings and sharply dressed people. When I asked Johnnie—by this time she had told me to drop the aunt—why everybody dressed like they were going to church, or juke joint, seeing as it was a Tuesday. She told me people there dressed like that every day. I was in the city now, where things were different. She told me, now that I was there, I had to dress the part and she would be taking me shopping the very next day. I was excited. I was going to get store-bought clothes, a far cry from the ones the neighbor woman made for me back home.

Once I got my new wardrobe—this is what Johnnie called my new clothes—she took me to have my hair done at a real beauty shop. I had never been to one of those either. Mama always washed my hair outside at the pump and pressed it at our kitchen stove. And when she did press it out, she made me pull it back into a ponytail with bangs; the only hairstyle I had ever had. Johnnie chose a new style for me, something similar to hers. She said I was a woman now and should look like one.

When we finally made it back to the brownstone, with the new clothes, shoes, and my new hairstyle, Johnnie shooed me upstairs to my room to change clothes. My room, or should I say rooms, was the whole second floor. Johnnie had given me the whole floor to frolic around in. Her rooms, as she put it, were on the third. I couldn't believe I had a whole floor to myself! When I was back home, I had a closet-sized room that was just big enough for a small bed and a small chest of drawers. Mama and me shared a closet at the back of the house, near the porch. I now had a bedroom nearly the size of Mama's house, with a closet and bath the size of Mama's bedroom, and furnished just as fancy as the rest of the house.

After changing clothes and looking at myself in the mirror, for what Johnnie said was an eternity, she took us out to dinner. We walked to a section of the city that was called Restaurant Row. There were eating places as far as the eye could see. Johnnie settled on an Ethiopian place that served food I had never heard of, let alone seen before. This was the first of many things that Johnnie had to show me about city life.

Over the course of time, she took me on a tour of the popular sights of the city, like the museums and Central

Park. We also visited a few jazz clubs. Jazz, like everything else there, was new to me, but I took to it right away. All I ever heard growing up were hymns and the Mississippi blues. I figured I had lived the blues long enough; I was due for a change.

Lastly, Johnnie took me to where she worked. When she left Mississippi, she got herself a job and put herself through college. From there she became a lawyer; opening her own practice in Harlem, near Strivers Row where she lived. That was how she was able to afford all of the nice things she had.

Johnnie said, if I was smart, I would follow in her footsteps and make a name for myself. I started by working as one of the assistants at her firm. Johnnie's practice had grown to the point she had taken on two new partners. This was unheard of back in those days by any woman, let alone a black woman. But people liked her, respected her, and that got her a long way. Johnnie said it didn't hurt none that she had a man's name either. When some folks came looking for a lawyer, looking for a man, and found her, they were shocked at first. But once she showed them what she could do, they soon got passed it.

I took to the office assistant job rather quickly. Back then we were called secretaries. I worked for Johnnie during the day and went to school at night. I went to school for business, to learn how to manage an office or anything else I wanted to manage. I graduated at the top of my class and soon became the office manager at Johnnie's firm. During that time, I met Kenny Brown. He was studying to be a lawyer just like Johnnie. She had taken him under her wing, teaching him the things you don't learn in school, but needed to know to get ahead.

Kenny and I started going out almost immediately. Before our first date, I knew I didn't know what to expect, so I turned to Johnnie. This was my first real date and I wanted to know how to conduct myself properly. Rubbing and squeezing Eddie Joe's dick on Mama's couch, didn't count as a date, or correct dating etiquette for that matter.

Johnnie asked me, what did Mama tell me about men? I told her nothing. Johnnie shook her head. She said it was just like her sister to be shy about human relations and men's bodies. So Johnnie told me everything that Mama wouldn't. I must say, I was dazed after our conversation. I had lots of questions and Johnnie had lots of answers. When it came to sex, (Johnnie explained that was what Mr.

Albert and Miss Sue were doing), I turned redder than a beet, because Johnnie gave me the full low down on that; no holds barred. She told me she could give me the technical version all day long, but until I felt it for myself, I wouldn't get it.

She was right. I didn't get it. I was twenty-two years old and I had never had sex; and when me and Kenny finally did it, it was terrible. I couldn't believe people actually thought that felt good. It hurt like hell and hurt like hell some more. I bled from him pushing inside me. Johnnie had warned this might happen. She even said there might be some pain, depending on how big he was. But nothing could have prepared me for what I went through. I never wanted to do that again.

When I got home and told Johnnie what happened. She laughed. She said Kenny was just as inexperienced as I was, and that's why it was so bad. Kenny didn't take his time to ease into me like Johnnie said he should have. He plowed into me like he was busting up a sod field. She told me, if I liked him well enough, I could stick with it and maybe it would get better. Well, I decided I didn't like him at all after that. We never went out again and he never asked me why. He soon moved on to another woman who worked in the office. I hoped she fared better than I did.

Still a Woman ~

It was another two years before I tried the sex stuff again. This time it was better.

His name was Rodrigo. Rodrigo was the owner of one of the restaurants Johnnie and I liked to frequent. He was handsome, suave, (a new word I picked up from one of the girls in the office), and by all standards back then, rich.

When he first started coming on to me, I didn't know what he was doing. You have to remember, I had only been out with one guy, Kenny. Once again, it took Johnnie to explain that the man was interested in me. So after she helped me figure that out, I started to flirt back, just like Johnnie taught me. After a few weeks of hits and misses, Rodrigo finally asked me out and I accepted.

He took me to a Latin club where he taught me how to do the salsa dance. That was the most fun I had ever had in my life. He was always a true gentleman; picking me up on time; taking me to the finest places; and treating me the way Johnnie said a woman wanted to be treated. I soon fell in love with Rodrigo, but this didn't last long. Rodrigo had a wife that he forgot to mention.

We were in his apartment one night, with him sexing me up pretty good, when this woman comes busting through the door, screaming and cursing at us in a language I had heard from Rodrigo, but didn't understand. I might not have understood the words, but I got the message, when she pointed at her wedding ring, as she screamed at us. While Rodrigo and his wife were yelling at each other, I gathered my clothes and ran for my life. I figured, once the woman got through yelling at him, she was coming for me.

When I told Johnnie what happened, she was fighting mad. The very next day, she marched right down to Rodrigo's restaurant and did some cursing and screaming of her own. Johnnie said, in situations like that, I could have been killed, had the woman had a gun or a knife. Rodrigo's dick may have been good, but not worth dying over. After that unpleasant incident, I wondered if I would ever get the hang of this man, woman thing.

Soon after the episode with Mr. and Mrs. Rodrigo, I got sick. I started throwing up and couldn't keep any food down. I was pregnant. Although I was green when it came to sex, Johnnie made sure I protected myself, by setting me up an appointment with her doctor for birth control, when I first started seeing Kenny. I took the pills as prescribed, but

Johnnie said, some men's sperm was stronger than the pill and evidently Rodrigo was one of those men.

Johnnie went with me to the "backroom" clinic, to get rid of the baby. She had asked me what I wanted to do about the situation. I didn't want to raise a child unmarried. And since Rodrigo already had a wife, there was no way he was going to marry me. Besides, even if he had married me, I would probably end up like Eva, when Eddie Joe ran off on her; alone, poor, and scared. I didn't want that.

Johnnie held my hand through the procedure and afterward took care of me. I sort of shut down after that. I didn't know what I was feeling or what I was supposed to feel. Johnnie, bless her heart, never tried to force me to talk about it. I learned later she couldn't talk about it either. The reason she never had any children, was because she had a botched abortion soon after she arrived in New York. Her pregnancy was one of the reasons she ran away from home. Her father had told them, if either she or Mama got pregnant before they got married, he would make them eat the baby. Johnnie didn't think he would make her eat it, but she feared he would beat it out of her. She said, maybe if Granddaddy had beaten it out of her, she still might have had children later on.

There was one thing Johnnie did say to me afterward. She said no matter what happened, I was still a woman and no one could take that away from me. I loved her for that because I had began to feel less than one.

A Better Woman ~

A couple of months after the baby was gone, I lost Mama.

Mama had been feeling poorly over the last couple of years but never told nobody. By the time she scraped up enough money, to go see the Black doctor over in the next town, it was too late. The cancer had spread over her body. There was nothing anybody could do.

I was angry. I wasn't angry because Mama died, I was angry because she didn't tell us she was sick. Me and Johnnie had to learn about it from Miss Sue after the fact. She was the one who called to tell us Mama was dead. Mama never told me nothing growing up, so I guess this was all part of it; just who she was. Mama kept her mouth shut right up to the very end.

When I started getting a paycheck, I would send Mama money every week. I told her to do some good things for herself or move into town into a better place. But Mama being mama used the money to help Eva with her child instead. I guess Mama was feeling guilty about sexing Eddie Joe, seeing as she continued to do so after he and Eva married. And not to mention she was probably old enough to be Eddie Joe's mama too.

In spite of it all, I was mad because all she had to do was call and tell me, and I would have been there to give her whatever she needed to get well.

When me and Johnnie went down for the funeral, I was shocked to see Mama's house had not changed one bit, since the day I left. She still had the same shabby couch and the same scarred furniture. Yes, I was angry at Mama, but I was also angry at myself. I was so busy living my life in the big city, I didn't make time to visit my mama. I was angry and ashamed.

When I cried at the funeral, it wasn't just because Mama was dead. I cried because I had neglected her and there was nothing I could do to make it up to her. She was gone. Johnnie tried consoling me the best she could. She said she had to share some of my guilt because Mama was her only sister. We both held each other and cried throughout the night.

#

When we got back after the funeral, I didn't know what to do with myself. I couldn't rest. I couldn't eat. Losing Mama that way hurt me, and I didn't know what to do with the hurt. I didn't bother Johnnie with my pain, because I knew she was dealing with pain of her own. She wished she would have been a better sister. Johnnie had tried to get Mama to move north with me, but Mama had refused. She said she wouldn't know how to live in a place like that. Mama said she was comfortable where she was. Johnnie said she wanted better for her sister, but Mama had to want better for herself. I guess she was right.

Johnnie eased her pain by throwing herself more into her work. I eased mine by getting my own brownstone, a few doors down from Johnnie. She hated to see me leave but understood I wanted my own place. She didn't blame me. She knew how it felt to have your own. I decided I needed my space to look inside myself, without another soul around. I wanted to improve myself and become a better woman. And sometimes that meant digging out all the pain and shame, which was never a pretty sight. I felt Johnnie needed to dig out hers too, without leaving witnesses.

#

After a few months of living in my new home, I met another man. His name was Logan Day. I met Logan at a conference that Johnnie insisted I attend. She said it would be good for me to network with other professionals in the city. This time Johnnie had the man checked out from top to bottom. She wanted to make sure he had no wife, no criminal past, or anything else that could come back to bite me. She didn't want me to get caught up in another incident like the one with Rodrigo.

Logan Day was a quiet man, but when he spoke, his voice and words were worth listening to. Logan was into real estate. He owned several buildings and shops around the city. I met him on the second day of the three-day conference. He and I were looking for a place in the back of the room, so we could pretend to listen to the featured speaker. He, like me, found the seminars boring but stayed just the same. We got acquainted during the break when he asked for my phone number. He didn't stay for the second half of the speech but promised to call and call he did.

Although Logan treated me like Rodrigo had, like a lady, there was a difference. He wasn't suave, which was just fine with me. I had had enough suave for a lifetime. Thank you very much. Logan was much more masculine about the whole thing. He was what Johnnie called a man's man; tall, handsome, and deep. His mind reached into the depths of things, pulling out understanding for all to comprehend—a word I learned from Logan. He was smart and made you want to be smart. I liked Logan a lot. So much so, I married him the following spring.

Johnnie was my maid of honor and Logan's brother Matthew stood up for him. Johnnie hosted the wedding and the reception at her home. She had it decorated so nicely, it made me teary. Johnnie was the best aunt and friend any woman could have. She and I both got teary when we thought how happy and excited Mama would have been to see all this.

Live flowers, candles, and ribbons occupied every conceivable surface. I wore an off-white lace gown that Johnnie had helped me pick out. I didn't think it was right to wear full-blown white, seeing as I wasn't a virgin. Logan looked so good in his dark suit. I was so proud to become his wife. Aside from liking him a whole lot, the man made me love him. He was just that good.

All of the people we knew from Johnnie's law firm attended, even Kenny. Aside from Logan's brother and some of his good friends, his parents attended, sitting proudly up front; looking on as we said our vows. I had met Logan's parents a few months earlier and we hit it off instantly. Mrs. Day, Logan's mother, had become like a mother to me and her husband became the father I never had. I felt special with these people.

Our wedding was beautiful, but our wedding night was like magic. Logan and I had agreed to wait until that night to love each other, and love each other we did. Logan was gentle and loving when we made love. He knew I wasn't experienced and took his time to touch me and teach me. That's when I learned the difference between sex and making love. What I had done with Kenny and Rodrigo couldn't have touched what was between Logan and me. It was so sweet I cried.

After our first night together, Logan showed me the other side of lovemaking. The side Mr. Albert and Miss Sue probably could have testified to, because he had me howling like a dog baying at the moon. I never knew anything could feel so good.

Johnnie told me, after that mess with Kenny, that sex could be mind-blowing. I didn't understand until Logan. My husband had me wanting him all the time. I couldn't wait 'til he got home from work each day. I would have dinner ready and after we ate…ooh wee! He would have me for dessert. That man would whisper dirty in my ear, having me coming like water from a faucet. My man wasn't deep for nothing!

A Child ~

Logan and I sexed so much we sexed right up on a baby, our first child.

When I started to get sick, like I did with Rodrigo, I knew instantly I was pregnant. I didn't want to tell Logan until I was a hundred percent sure. I made an appointment with my doctor who confirmed it. Me and Logan were having a baby!

That evening, as usual, I had dinner prepared. But this time, instead of saving dessert for later, I made Logan's favorite cake. Right away he wanted to know the occasion. We had celebrated our first year of marriage a month before, so he knew it wasn't that. I told him it was a surprise and that I would tell him later when we were in bed.

Usually, Logan was the one doing all the whispering during our romps, but this time, I did a little whispering of my own. I waited until we got in bed, and he was deep inside me, to inform him he was going to be a father. You would have thought that man had won all the money in the world, he was grinning so proudly. Logan loved me special that night.

#

When it was time for the baby to come, Logan was a nervous wreck. It took me and Johnnie to calm him down. When it got close to my due date, Logan had started working from the house. I was glad because this was our first child and I was just as nervous and scared as he was. He was in his office when my water broke. I calmly called Johnnie, then walked into the office to give him the news. Logan nearly fell out of his chair when I told him.

By the time Johnnie got to our house—we still lived down the street from her—the first pain had struck. This sent Logan into a tailspin. He was hyperventilating so bad that when the ambulance came, Johnnie had to calm him, to keep them from putting him on a stretcher. Logan finally got it together long enough to accompany me to the hospital. Johnnie met us there.

When the baby came and the nurse placed her in Logan's arms. He had his chest stuck out so far, you would have thought he had pushed that baby out himself. He had gotten so attached to her, that he refused to give her back for the lady to clean her up, and so they let him do it. The doctors and nurses in the delivery room had a good laugh that day. Except for our wedding day, I had never seen my husband prouder than when he was holding Amber. Our baby girl's full name was Amber Nicole Day. Amber was Logan's mother's middle name and Nicole was mama's. Mrs. Day couldn't stop crying she was so honored. The first time she held her namesake, me and Logan both knew that baby was going to be spoiled rotten.

#

Exactly six weeks after Amber was born, Logan wanted to show her off, so we invited a few people over for a get-together. Mrs. Day offered to have the affair catered, in exchange for inviting some of her friends to ooh and ah over her first grandchild. So needless to say, what started out as a small gathering had turned into a full-blown party. People were everywhere. And you know Johnnie; she had to get into the act by adding her decorating touches here and there. The best thing that came out of that party was Amber receiving tons of clothes, diapers, and anything else a baby needed. I was feeling just as proud as any parent could be. My baby girl was well-loved.

While everyone was eying baby Amber, I took a breather in the kitchen alone. I guess you could say I was overwhelmed with being a new mother and needed a minute to myself. I was just standing there, looking out the window into the backyard, when I felt a presence behind me. I turned to find Jonathon Allen, Logan's best friend, at my back. Jonathon was supposed to stand up for Logan at our wedding, but was out of the country and wasn't able to get back in time. He had shown up a week later to give his congratulations. He and Logan were close and he was the first person Logan called to share the news that he was going to be a father.

Jonathon was a fine man. One that made women's hearts race and panties wet—including mine. Tall and handsome, he turned heads instantly. When Logan first introduced us, he gave me that special feeling between my legs, but I quickly shoved it aside. You had to hurry up and put the devil in his place before he got his toe in the door. I was married to a wonderful man and there was no way I was going to mess that up, fine man or not.

I hadn't known Jonathon had followed me into the kitchen until I found him standing there. He had come in so quiet like. It was like he was sneaking in. I asked him if he needed something. Nervous, because of my carnal feelings, I headed to the refrigerator to get him a drink, when he grabbed my arm to stop me. He told me I was the only thing that he wanted.

Well, you could have knocked me over with a feather I was so stunned. I was too stunned to react. I knew I was attracted to him, but didn't know he felt the same about me. He had really caught me off guard. And it didn't help that the man was eying me like I didn't have a stitch of clothes on. You could almost see what he was thinking. It was just that clear, as to what he wanted. Pulling my arm free of his fingers, I wanted to cover myself. In his mind, Jonathon Allen was already inside me. I was about to give him a piece of my mind when Johnnie came into the kitchen.

Evidently, Jonathon didn't want an audience to his backstabbing, because he mumbled something and quickly vacated the room, with Johnnie giving him the evil eye as he passed her. She told me she'd watched him lick his chops over me all afternoon. She said the man was no good and bore watchin' and closely. He was no true friend of Logan's. I agreed.

The rest of the evening went without a hitch. Everyone had gotten their fill of baby Amber and left us with well wishes for the future. After the last person left, (which was Johnnie; she wanted to make sure Jonathon wasn't hiding in the house somewhere), we put our beautiful baby girl to bed and retired to our room to practice making another.

Trouble ~

It would be months before my sleep pattern would get to the point, where I could get some rest.

Amber was up every couple of hours, every night like clockwork, wanting a tit or to be changed. I was glad I decided to breastfeed, that way I could put my nipple in her mouth and doze off again. This mama thing was wearing me down.

I had to give it to my husband though, he was a great dad. The moment he hit the door from work, he would take the baby for the rest of the evening. Daddy and daughter would sit and coo at each other and smile. That man loved his daughter. During these times, I would lie down for a while and catch a nap. Logan was the one to suggest this. He saw how tired I would be when he got home. And although he couldn't feed Amber, he was the one who got up to change her during the night.

I was glad he talked me into being a stay-at-home mother because I would not have been any good torn between two places. Johnnie was sorry to see me go but was happy for our little family. And it wasn't like I didn't get to see her; she still dropped by at least three times a week, mostly when Logan was at work. She said no single woman, old or young, needed to be hanging out with a married woman when her husband was at home. That only brought trouble. Johnnie knew I could trust her, but she was set in her ways and said right was right, family or not. She also said, sometimes family and friends would do you wrong before people in the street. Mama used to say that too.

Well, somebody didn't teach this way of thinking to Jonathon, because he started hanging around quite often. It all started when Logan invited him to dinner one evening. One dinner turned into dinner every other evening. This didn't sit well with Johnnie and she told me so. I told her that I didn't like it either, but what could I do? He was Logan's best friend. She told me to never be alone with the man, and never entertain him when Logan wasn't home.

Well, the devil must have heard Johnnie's advice, because he plotted up on a scheme for Jonathon to drop by when Logan wasn't home. I was in the kitchen washing dishes when I heard Logan tell Jonathon he could come by the next day, to get some papers he was preparing for him. I wasn't worried until he gave him the time; around noon, well before he got home.

This caught in my brain, but I decided not to borrow trouble. This was one of Mama's favorite sayings. I told myself, the incident at Amber's party was a one-time thing, and that Jonathon probably was ashamed of himself for acting that way. I let myself believe this because he had been a perfect gentleman the evenings he had dinner with us. There wasn't a wayward eye or stray hand during those times. I foolishly believed he was sorry for what he had done.

I shouldn't have listened to that false voice, because it had lulled me into a false state of being. The next day when Jonathon came by, I had the papers he needed right there on the table at the front door. I didn't want to give him a reason to come inside. He rang the bell. I answered; gave him a polite smile as I handed him the papers, and he left. I held my breath the whole time and released it when I closed the door. That wasn't so bad.

While I was patting myself on the back, congratulating myself on a job well done, the devil was laying the trap for round two. Whereas I had my guard up the first round, I was totally unprepared for the second.

It had been a month since Jonathon had come for those papers, or been by for dinner. That was a relief for both me and Johnnie. We thought the man had repented and moved on. I even asked Logan about him, and he told me Jonathon had been busy with work and was preparing to leave the country for a three-month stay to further his business overseas. I even found out he had a new lady friend in his life and had plans to take her with him.

I was grinning with relief. Although I loved my husband, I must admit, my body had a certain longing for that man and the devil knew it. Why else would he keep throwing that fine man in my face? Johnnie knew it too and told me to be ever so cautious, so I wouldn't find myself in a hot pot, roastin', if I yielded to temptation. She said the devil had a funny way of making you do things you say you would never do.

I had just put Amber down for her afternoon nap when the bell rang. I ran downstairs to open the door—to Jonathon. I wasn't dressed for company. I wasn't shabby or anything, I just didn't want to receive company in a low-cut top and shorts; especially not his company. It was a hot day and I had planned to clean the house while the baby was

asleep, and saw no need to put on anything different.
Besides, I wasn't expecting anyone to come calling.

Jonathon said Logan had left another set of papers
on his desk, and that he needed them before he left town
that evening. I told him Logan didn't mention any papers or
him stopping by. He said it was a last-minute thing, so he
probably forgot to tell me.

I was a little uncertain, but let him in to wait in the
sitting room, while I went to Logan's office to look for the
papers. One thing about Logan's desk, it was always junky,
with papers scattered everywhere. Whenever I had the time,
I would organize everything for him. Remember, I was an
office manager, so managing my husband's office was a
snap.

Looking everywhere and not finding any papers, I
was about to return to the door to tell Jonathon I didn't see
them when I felt him pressed against my backside. I didn't
even hear him come into the room. Before I could protest,
he reached around under my shirt and cupped my titties, as
he pressed himself deeper into me.

I froze. I think he took this as consent, because he
quickly slid one hand down into the front of my shorts,

beneath my panties, until he had a finger inside me. He started gyrating against me from behind, all the while working that finger in and out; rubbing it against my button. He stuck his tongue in my ear, whispering how he was going to fuck me and how good it was going to be.

I opened my mouth to say no, but nothing came out. At the same time, I wasn't sure I wanted to say no because I had let myself have fantasies about him. My mind was mixed up; I couldn't think. My mind didn't want to deal with what was happening, but I forced it to. This was no time for it to skip out on me.

While I was trying to wrestle my mind into action, he bent me over the desk. Reality tried to hit home when I heard his zipper slide down. It was one thing to have fantasies, but it was quite another to have to deal with the real thing. He still had his finger inside me and working it faster. My body betrayed me by getting wet; getting aroused. My nipples were standing out from his touch. In my mind's eye, I could see Jonathon sticking himself in me and pumping away from behind—and me letting him, if I didn't do something quick.

This thought brought anger. That me letting him part, pushed me into action. I bucked wildly against him when he tried to pull my shorts down. But before he could accomplish this, I spotted a pair of scissors on my husband's desk. If I had cleaned his office that morning, instead of waiting for Amber to nap, those scissors would have been in a drawer where they belonged; in a drawer where I couldn't reach them.

I grabbed the scissors and with all my strength, freed myself from him. I placed the sharp points of my weapon to his throat. I walked him backward to the front door with those scissors sticking him; applying pressure when he didn't move fast enough. When we got to the door, I opened it and between clenched teeth, told him I would kill him if I ever saw him again. That man turned and ran like the wind.

I never laid eyes on Jonathon Allen again. Logan said he had moved his whole operations somewhere overseas; saying he liked living there over home. I didn't care what the reason was, I meant what I said. I would kill him. I was still angry about what happened that day. But I wasn't just angry at him, I was angry at myself for almost letting lust get the better of me.

I never told Logan what happened in his office that day. There was no way I could, with the part I played in it. When he didn't mention Jonathon stopping by—for those make-believe papers—I knew then, it was Jonathon's scam for getting inside the house all along. He knew Logan was at work and he would have me right where he wanted me— so he thought.

The next time I saw Johnnie, she knew something was wrong when she asked about Jonathon, and without warning, I broke down sobbing. She held me while I told her everything, between hiccupping sobs. I didn't allow myself to cry the day it happened or any day for that matter. I thought if I cried, it would somehow give that whole situation some sort of power over me, and I couldn't allow that to happen.

But there was another reason I hadn't cried. I knew if I had been just a little bit weaker that day, I would have given in to him. I would have let him spread me across my husband's desk and let him have his way with me.

But I wasn't weak. I fought for my husband, my marriage, my soul.

More Trouble ~

Not long after that trouble with Jonathon Allen, a new problem blew into town, in the form of Eva Todd, my best friend from back home.

After Mama died, I continued what she started, by sending Eva money to help out. I guess you can say I have a little bit of mama in me after all. I felt sorry for Eva. Her folks did the best they could in helping, but they didn't have much themselves. Once Eddie Joe ran off, he never bothered to send money or anything that could feed or dress them.

Eva showed up on my doorstep one Saturday, while Logan was out of town. Johnnie had stopped by to gossip about the new neighbors who had moved in next door to her. It seemed they liked to party all the time, with loud music and strange visitors at all hours of the night. This didn't sit too well with Johnnie. She was preparing to have them served with papers, for disorderly conduct or something to that effect. This was one of the perks of being a lawyer.

It was a nice day, so we decided to sit out on the stoop with Amber and enjoy the activity of the neighborhood. We hadn't been sitting long when a cab stopped at my house. I wasn't expecting anyone, and Logan wasn't due back until the next day. As soon as the back door opened and Eva Todd got out, Johnnie frowned. She didn't know her, had only seen her once before that day, but she frowned.

When I recognized the woman as Eva, I passed my baby to Johnnie and flew down the steps to greet her. We hugged and cried because we hadn't seen each other since Mama's funeral. I walked her back up the steps to greet Johnnie, while the cabbie gathered her bags. Johnnie took Eva's offered hand, but the frown never left her face. I filed that away to ask her about her behavior later.

It seemed that Eva had gotten kicked out of her rental house after her son, Eddie Joe Jr, left. One of Miss Sue's relatives had taken to the boy and took him to Missouri to finish raising him. The boy was smart, smart enough for somebody to want to pay his way for better living and learning.

I still sent Eva money from time to time, but not on the regular; like when her son was still at home. Mama always said all grown folks should fend for themselves, and

Johnnie seconded that. But I had no idea things had gotten that bad for her until she showed up that day. She told how things went from bad to worse and how she was grateful that Eddie Joe Jr. didn't have to witness it. We sat on that stoop, chatting and laughing like old times. All the while, Johnnie bounced Amber on her knee, never taking her eyes off of Eva.

We finally moved the reunion inside for dinner. Before Eva arrived, Johnnie claimed she was too busy to stay. All that changed the moment Eva set foot inside my house with her suitcases. Eva kept looking around in wonder, saying how I had done well for myself. She picked up a photo of me and Logan with baby Amber. She went on about my husband's good looks, and how fine he was. Johnnie's eyes narrowed at how she drew out the word fine, in relation to my husband.

Johnnie and I played hostesses; cooking dinner, while Eva played with the baby and caught me up on what was going on back home. It seemed that things hadn't changed much since I left. People were still receiving very little education and working the fields as before. This made me sad. It also made me sad that once Eva got pregnant and married, she had become one of those who were undereducated; dropping out of school to play mother and short-term wife.

When the conversation slowed down, Johnnie finally spoke up. She had grown quiet the second Eva got out of that cab. She asked Eva what were her plans, making a point of staring at her shabby suitcases when she asked this. I thought Johnnie was being rude, but held my tongue. I had known her long enough to know there was always a method and reasoning behind her questions. I trusted her.

Eva said she hoped she could stay with me and Logan a while until she could get on her feet. Johnnie's mouth tightened with this answer. She asked her why she didn't let me know she was coming. Well, Eva didn't have a ready answer for that one. I don't think she expected to come up against the likes of Johnnie. With this question, Eva looked around nervous like, and then she started to cry. I felt sorry for her and gave her a comforting hug. Johnnie rolled her eyes, calling her Evil under her breath.

Problem Solved ~

Eva stayed with me that first night and we had a ball.

After Johnnie went home, and Amber was down for the night, we drank glasses of wine and reminisced over younger days. We talked about playing in the woods and the corn fields and how we used to peek in on her folks. We even talked about Eddie Joe. Eva said after he ran off, she started back using her maiden name because she didn't feel married. Mr. Albert tried to find Eddie Joe at one time, but couldn't. Eva's daddy wished she had chosen a better man to play house with.

The next morning I heard voices coming from downstairs. Amber was still asleep in her crib, so I put on my housecoat and went down to see who was talking. It was Eva and Logan. He had come home to find Eva making coffee in our kitchen. I was about to make the introductions, but Eva had beat me to it. She had already explained to Logan why she was there and for how long she would be. Her staying with us was fine with him.

What wasn't fine with me though, was how Eva was dressed. The nightgown she wore was thin, to say the least. I asked her where was her housecoat and she said she didn't have one. I politely took off mine and gave it to her. My husband had seen me naked, so it didn't matter if my night clothes were uncovered, but for Eva, that didn't sit right with me. And it didn't sit right with Logan either, because he was looking anywhere but at her.

Johnnie came by before she headed off to work. She said she wanted to see how things were going with Evil being in the house. I tried to correct her about Eva's name, but she didn't pay me no mind. I was glad Eva was upstairs while we talked. I didn't want her to think Johnnie didn't like her, even though I knew she didn't. I told Johnnie how I found Eva making coffee for Logan this morning with no housecoat on, so I was going to take her shopping for one, and maybe a couple of dresses for job hunting.

You would have thought I had slapped Johnnie with the way she reacted. She told me to have Evil all packed up and ready this evening when she stopped by after work. She was moving her in with her. I tried telling her it was fine for Eva to stay with us, but Johnnie said it was best she stayed at her house until she got on her feet. She would have more room to move around. Besides, she reminded me of the single women, married couple rule. Single women had no business keeping company with a married couple. I guess she was right, even though I trusted Eva.

When I told Eva she would be staying with Johnnie, it was like her heart fell or something. She said she didn't think Johnnie liked her and wouldn't feel comfortable staying with her. After I told her she would be having a whole floor to herself, and not just a room, she perked up a bit. She liked the sound of having rooms instead of a room.

Eva was all packed and ready when Johnnie came for her. Logan helped them with Eva's belongings. He said he was glad to help. The truth be told, I think he was more uncomfortable with Eva in the house than he let on; maybe more so than Johnnie. I don't think he liked finding an underdressed woman in his kitchen that wasn't his wife.

Although Eva lived with Johnnie, we saw each other every day. Eva would go job hunting in the mornings then come to our house for lunch. Sometimes she would stay for dinner. On these nights, Johnnie would make it her business to have dinner with us too. She said she needed to keep an eye on ol' Evil. I wished Johnnie would warm up to Eva. She felt about her the way Mama did when she was alive.

Eva soon found her a job as a telephone operator. She worked the night shift. Johnnie was glad, not because she would be able to find her own place soon, but she said it would keep Evil busy. If she was busy, she wouldn't have time to stir up trouble. Frankly, I didn't get why she still disliked Eva so much. She hadn't caused any trouble. I thought they were getting along better and was hoping they would become close like Johnnie and I were, but that never happened.

Everything was going fine until I started feeling uncomfortable in my own skin. This went on until it was too powerful to ignore. So instead of trying to overlook it or fight it, I just waited for whatever it was to come to light. Mama always said, what's done in the dark always crawls out from the shadows for all to see.

Trouble Doubles Back ~

I got up that morning feeling something was terribly wrong and had been for some time. I just couldn't put my finger to it.

Nobody was sick. After Mama died the way she did, I made Johnnie promise not to keep anything like that from me and she said she wouldn't. Logan was feeling fine because he was singing in the shower as usual. I had taken Amber in for a checkup only a week before, so I knew whatever was wrong, it wasn't with her.

While Logan bathed and dressed Amber, I went downstairs to start breakfast. This was our routine every morning. Nothing was out of place there. Not able to pinpoint the problem, I shook it off and continued with my day, which included meeting Eva later. She was working steadily and wanted to go shopping to buy more suitable clothes for work. She worked nights and usually slept during the day, but said she would stay awake for the shopping trip.

After kissing my husband goodbye, I got dressed for the day's outing. It was a fine day to be out and about too. The sun was shining, just inviting you to come out and enjoy it. I put Amber in her stroller and off we went.

Amber loved being outside in the sunshine and babbled the whole time she and I walked down to Johnnie's.

Letting myself and Amber inside Johnnie's house, I rolled my eyes because the place was still, which meant Eva wasn't up and about. Never once did I think twice about letting myself into Johnnie's house unannounced. She told me, after I left for my own place, I could still come and go as I pleased.

Sleepy or not, Eva was going shopping whether she liked it or not. It was the only day I could set aside to go with her. I left Amber sleeping in her stroller, (fresh air always made her sleepy) and marched right up those stairs. I was hoping she wasn't asleep, because it usually took Eva forever to get ready to go anywhere, with all her primping. You would have thought she was going to enter a beauty contest instead of buying some clothes.

The closer I got to Eva's bedroom, I heard noises; some familiar noises. As I stood outside the door listening, that feeling of something wrong had taken me by the throat and was squeezing. I could hardly breathe. Not wanting to, but needing to, I opened the door to the sight of my life; my husband pounding away inside my best friend! They were going at it so tough, they didn't know I was in the room until I started screaming.

Logan jumped off of Eva like somebody set his backside on fire. He scrambled off that bed sputtering; trying to pull on his pants like that was going to solve something. I paced around the room confused; still screaming; wanting to know why.

While Logan was trying to put his pants on and calm me down, Eva propped herself up against the headboard like she was watching one of her daytime stories on the television. She actually had a grin on her face. My best friend had set me up to catch her fucking my husband! Johnnie and Mama were right. They knew all along the woman was evil. Either I didn't see it or just didn't want to see it. I never figured out which.

Not able to handle any more tussling with Logan or Eva's evil grin, I ran downstairs, grabbed my baby from her stroller, and fled Johnnie's house. I didn't want to take the time to push the stroller, because I thought it would slow me down. Besides, in the state I was in, I might have turned it over and hurt my child in the process. There had been enough hurtin' for one day.

I started crying the moment my feet hit the sidewalk. Amber looked into my face and started crying too. She didn't know why she was crying, only that she should, because her mama was crying. I walked and we cried until I got to Johnnie's office. By the time I got to the front of the building, she had met me at the door. One of her assistants had seen me heading that way in a state and ran ahead to tell Johnnie. Johnnie asked no questions, she just hailed a cab and took us home.

I didn't realize we were back at my house until I was sitting on my couch still clutching a crying Amber. Johnnie had to pry my arms from her. I didn't want to let go, because only Amber shared my pain. After she got Amber quieted down, Johnnie took her upstairs for a nap, so she could tend to me. She knew whatever happened, it was bad.

After she pieced the story together, through my hysterics, she was fit to be tied. She snatched up my telephone and made two calls. I was too upset to understand what was being said to the people on the other end. Everything was all cloudy. The last thing I remembered was lying in my bed. I found out later, Johnnie had called a friend of hers to watch over me and Amber,

while she handled things at her house. But by the time she
got there, both Eva and Logan were gone. She doubled
back to my house, this time with her pistol. She was hoping
Logan was stupid enough to show up there. The second
person she called was her personal assistant, to be on
standby with bail money, just in case she caught up with
either of them.

For two days I stayed in bed, unable to function.
Johnnie let me grieve. She took good care of me and
Amber. It was a good thing Amber was on solid food
because I don't think I could have fed her. Logan and Eva
had taken away all my strength.

On the third day, I was so sick I couldn't stay in
bed. My stomach wouldn't let me. Johnnie said it was
nerves over what happened. But after I couldn't keep food
down for a fifth day, she took me to see my doctor. I was
pregnant. This brought fresh pain to my world. My husband
was gone and I would have to raise two children on my
own.

Logan turned up two weeks later, while Johnnie
was at work. He knew she was gunning for him, so he
made sure she wasn't around when he let himself in the

house that morning. I was feeding Amber when I felt his presence in the kitchen.

He looked bad like he hadn't slept in days. He stood there not knowing what to say or where to start. He told me he was sorry and he didn't mean for any of that to happen. He never meant to hurt me he said. I found out he'd been sleeping with Eva almost from the time she got there. He told me that morning I found them in the kitchen is when it started. Evil, (I had started calling her that now too), had invited him to touch her and he did. He said it was like something had taken over him and he couldn't fight it.

Tears ran down my face while I listened to him. He talked on and on, with me waiting. I was waiting for him to get to the part about fixing it and starting over, but that part never came; that was not why he was there. He came to get his things; he wanted to be with Eva.

I guess I didn't have any more shock left in me, because I didn't even flinch. I watched him leave the kitchen to head upstairs to get his stuff. I was still standing in the same spot when he came back to kiss Amber. She reached for her daddy with a smile. She had no idea he was leaving her. One day that smile would be a frown whenever his name came up. Logan placed some papers on the kitchen table, said some words I didn't hear, and left. He didn't even give me a chance to tell him about the baby. At this point, I don't think he would have cared. Evil had him by the dick.

I finished feeding my baby girl and laid her down. I went back to the spot I stood in when Logan left and I cried, hard. Not because I lost my husband. I cried because I had defended my marriage against his best friend, only to have mine destroy it. I cried because I should have given in to temptation that day and let Jonathon fuck my brains out.

That was the last time I saw my husband.

Johnnie went into overdrive filing papers, any papers that were going to bury him, as she put it. I let her do whatever she wanted. The only thing I wanted to focus on was taking care of my children.

A New Day ~

I bounced back from my husband leaving me for that cow Evil pretty quick. I didn't have time for a pity party, as Mama would have called it. I was pregnant, with a small child to feed and raise.

Mr. and Mrs. Day were devastated when they heard what their son had done to his family. Mrs. Day was over almost every day, doing things for me and Amber. I guess she was trying to make amends for what her son had done. I didn't blame her or Mr. Day. Logan was a grown-ass man and was responsible for himself. Matthew, Logan's brother, would come by from time to time to sit and play with Amber. I guess he felt guilty too.

Soon the time came and I had Brianna. This time Logan wasn't there to hold his daughter with his chest stuck out. Johnnie was there with me, with Mr. and Mrs. Day in the waiting room. I tried not to think about Logan's absence, while I pushed my beautiful baby girl from my body. It wouldn't have done any good anyway.

#

Time marched on and we marched on with it. A year had passed and still no word from Logan. At least he never contacted me. Mr. Day said they heard from him from time to time. Always apologizing, but never sorry enough to come home to take care of his family. Matthew tried to hang around more often, trying to fill the hole his brother left until I stopped him. He couldn't pay his brother's debt, no matter how hard he tried, so why try?

It didn't matter. Me and the girls had everything we needed. Johnnie made sure of that. The only thing she couldn't accomplish was a divorce. I wouldn't sign the papers. I didn't sign them, because I refused to give that evil bitch the satisfaction of being Mrs. Day. That's what she wanted most of all and I'm sure she cursed me every day because I wouldn't give it to her.

At first, Johnnie disagreed with me not signing the papers, but once she saw the punishment in it, she grinned like a proud mama. She said it was about time some of her rubbed off on me. Despite not being divorced, Johnnie made sure I wouldn't have to work again unless I wanted to. That suited me just fine. I needed to be available around the clock to protect my babies. The world had proven to be cruel no matter how good you tried to be, and I wanted to defend my girls from its harsh licks as best I could.

After the fog wore off, me and the girls were laughing again. Amber had stopped crying and asking for her daddy, without me having to tell her to. I guess even in her little mind, she knew he wasn't coming back. With Brianna never knowing him, made things that much easier. Although I knew one day I would have to explain him to her; explain him to both of my girls. The thing was, I had no clue how I was going to do that. How do you tell your children their daddy left because he couldn't control his dick?

Pay Back ~

Logan had been gone four good years when two policemen showed up at my door. They asked if they could speak with Mrs. Louise Day. That was me.

Johnnie happened to be visiting that day and went right into lawyer mode, taking over completely. She asked them why they were there. I think she thought I was in some kind of trouble, but I took one look at their faces and could see this wasn't so. They seemed real uncomfortable about being there.

After Johnnie finally gave in and let them into the house, they informed us that my husband had died. After they told me, I guess they thought I was going to fall apart or something, but that wasn't the case. I was done grieving over that man long ago. There were no more tears I needed or wanted to shed. I think even Johnnie expected me to fall away in a dead faint. It didn't happen.

After everyone silently agreed I was ok, with the subject of my husband being dead, Johnnie asked the question I wanted to ask but was unsure if I even cared enough to want to know the answer. How did he die?

Well, those two men really got uncomfortable then. They heed and hawed awhile. I guess trying to find the more polite words to say. One of them finally told us what the official report said. Mr. Logan Day died of an aneurysm, while his live-in girlfriend, Eva Todd, was performing fellatio on him. In other words, a vein burst in his head while Evil was sucking his dick.

Once again, everybody in the room waited for the expected fallout that never came. Though, I guess there was some fallout, but not what they were looking for. They were maybe expecting tears or outrage, but what they got was laughter.

I started laughing and couldn't stop. I laughed so hard, I doubled over with tears washing my face. After I could calm down some, I looked at Johnnie and told her, Evil blew his mind. Well, she found this funny too. We both laughed hard at this. We were thinking of the time she told me sex could be mind-blowing. Well, it couldn't have happened to a more deserving man.

We were still laughing when the policemen left my house, scratching their heads and all red-faced. They thought we had lost our minds.

We had the funeral, which the Days insisted they take care of. They said it was the least they could do. I guess they were still feeling guilty about Logan and probably a little embarrassed too, seeing as how he died. The girls didn't show much emotion. This surprised me about Amber. I was expecting her to tear up or something, but I guess she was young enough to have forgotten him when he left. I guess this was a good thing. Me? I took it like a champ. Like I said, I had no more tears for the man.

After the funeral, Johnnie went through all of Logan's papers and said it was a good thing I never divorced him. His dying made me a very rich woman with all his real estate holdings and such. I had enough money to live good and pass along to my girls when I died. At least he was good for something.

A few days after I put my husband into the ground, Evil returned. She had the nerve to show up at my door, talking about how sorry she was for all that happened. She had her hat in hand, as Mama used to say. I let her in. I wanted to know the real reason she was there. Plus, I had some things I needed to get off my chest, so to speak.

Well, it didn't take long before she got to the point. She was broke and looking for a handout. When Logan died, he died without a will, which left her with nothing. She didn't even own the house she was living in. It was in Logan's name. And since it was part of his estate and I was his wife, it now belonged to me. The day after we found out Logan was dead, Johnnie had the floozy served with eviction papers, promptly throwing her backstabbing behind into the street.

Miss Evil thought she had hit the jackpot once Logan left me, so she quit her job. She had no money of her own, only whatever money Logan gave her. Money she should have saved for a rainy day, she used to live the high life; buying the finest of clothes and such. Well, now it was storming and she was caught unsheltered. I guess she thought Logan was going to live forever.

I let her put on her sob story and talk for a while. Then I calmly and without warning, commenced to whooping her trifling ass! I whooped her so, my girls got scared and ran down to Johnnie's for help. They had never seen their mama act like that before. It was always Johnnie coming out of a bag on folks, not me.

By the time Johnnie got there, Evil was looking to beg anybody for help, even Johnnie. She had to pull me off of her before I killed her.

Fearful that Evil might call the law on me, Johnnie had a doctor friend of hers come to the house to patch her up. When she and the doctor were satisfied the woman would live, (but not without more than a few mental and physical scars), Johnnie took Evil to her house. She came back an hour later with the still shaken girls. Johnnie had paid the tramp off. She gave her twenty thousand dollars, put her in a cab, and warned her, if she ever returned, she would finish the job I had started.

It was over. Everyone was in their proper place; the girls and I in our home, Logan in his grave, and Eva Todd ran out of town.

The End of the Road ~

Things went back to normal after Eva left. I gave her back her name after I got my satisfaction.

My girls grew up and had girls of their own. Johnnie sold her practice and started traveling all over the world. She said there were places she wanted to see before she died. She had three good years of exploring before she came back home sick. Like Mama, she had cancer. By the time she realized something was wrong, it was too late. This time it was me taking care of her.

We spent her last days reminiscing over our lives. I asked her why she never married. Johnnie said she tried in her young woman days to catch herself a husband. But once the potential grooms found she couldn't give them children, they just faded away like smoke. After a while, she just stopped trying. She did say she had a man friend she saw from time to time, to "touch her up". We laughed at that.

The day Johnnie died was the saddest day of my life. Johnnie Mae was more than a friend to me, she was my second mama and I missed her. My best friend was gone.

#

Now here I lay; waiting on my turn to leave this earth. The same thing that took Mama and Johnnie away, would soon claim me.

There go my girls again; all wide-eye and teary, peeping in on me. They're sad, but I told them not to be. I had a full life, a good life. And I gave them all I had to give to make them better women than me.

When I raised my children, I set out on the task of educating them on things they could never learn in school. I gave my girls culture, and interests in many things. We even took trips to different cities, to different states, to let them see there were other places besides the city they lived in. I wanted them to have choices, choices that didn't necessarily include marrying and settling down with a man.

Don't get me wrong, I don't have anything against marriage, marriage is fine for folks who can make it work. It just seemed that me and Mama weren't two of those folks. Both our husbands ran off on us. I just wanted my girls to know there was a whole big world out there and they could navigate it any way they chose to. There were no restraints.

When I thought about how restraining some people could be with their children, I thought about Mama. I didn't want my girls to grow up dumb as dirt like me. I was the type of mama who told my girls about everything, no matter how hard the subject. I felt if Mama had been straightforward with me, Eva wouldn't have taken my husband or at least I would have seen her for what she was.

There were a lot of things Mama should have told me. Dealing with men should have been front and center. Johnnie said, yeah, she should have told me more than she did, but she didn't think Mama knew much. Their mama never told them nothing either. She said, had their mama told them the truth of where babies came from, and what the consequences were of getting pregnant without a husband, maybe she wouldn't have gotten pregnant in the first place. Johnnie said she still would have left home, but that wouldn't have been the deciding factor. She said her mama told them a stork brought babies. We laughed. It seemed silly, but Mama never told me that much.

I told Johnnie to not think her sister was all that naïve. I told her about the time I saw her in bed with Eddie Joe. Johnnie had a good laugh on that one. She didn't think her sister had it in her. All this time, she thought Mama was living a celibate life. Johnnie wondered who else mama was screwing.

Although Mama didn't tell me much, I loved her and I learned from her not saying anything. I learned to be more forthcoming with my own girls. When I was through, I wanted them to know how to handle a man, handle life. But they took their own route.

Like I said in the beginning, I tried to give them my wisdom as I learned it, in hopes they would learn from my experiences without having to repeat the mistakes. But you know, I guess they did listen and learned, but not the way I expected them to. They took everything I gave them about men to heart and used it all against them. Amber and Brianna took no prisoners when it came to their relationships. They dogged men every which way they could. This really makes me sad. I never meant for that to happen. I just wanted them to be more vigilant in their relationships; not have the 'get them before they get me' attitude. Two wrongs don't make a right.

So I leave this legacy for my granddaughters, who are about the age I was when I first peered in on Mr. Albert and Miss Sue doing the do. I want them to be better women and know more than somebody telling them to keep their dress tail down.

And maybe, just maybe, they will avoid the Eddie Joes, Jonathon Allens, and the Logan Days of the world, and find true happiness with men who are right, good, and faithful.

***

*This is my first published novella and I hope you enjoyed, **Mama Said, Keep Your Dress Tail Down.***
Women who grew up in the rural South back in the day may have heard those very words from an adult female, whether it was their mother, grandmother, or aunt. I know I sure did. And like Mama Lou. I hadn't a clue, as to what those words meant. I was an adult myself when I figured it all out. So this story is somewhat my story, as with anyone else who can relate.
I want to thank you for allowing me to take up a little of your time, to share with you this short but sweet story.
Thank you,

Olivia M. Dutton

www.ingramcontent.com/pod-product-compliance
Lightning Source LLC
Chambersburg PA
CBHW061452170626
46811CB00004B/1470